The General C

Beard

GW00382598

Philippe de Vosjoli
Robert Mailloux

Table of Contents

INTRODUCTION

For those without experience in popular herpetology, Australians have given the name "dragon" to many of their native lizards in the subfamily Agaminae. Thus, Australia has lizards called water dragons, netted dragons, chameleon dragons, and the currently very popular bearded dragons.

During the first half of the 1980's, several species of bearded dragons were imported into the U.S. from Germany and, in several instances, probably as animals illegally smuggled out of Australia (see Hoser 1993). These lizards, with their attractive looks and delightfully docile personalities, charmed many herpetoculturists, including the authors, who obtained their first animals, supposedly captive-bred in Germany, from U.S. reptile dealers in 1984. The authors subsequently set out to captive breed these species and were the first to develop large-scale captive propagation of bearded dragons in the U.S., having bred and distributed several thousand animals since their initial endeavors.

For those of you who have not yet been exposed to these lizards, be aware that they rank among the very best of lizard pets. A moderate-size animal, they have pleasing form, attractive pattern and coloration, and make an impressive display in a well-designed vivarium. Bearded dragons also demonstrate a variety of interesting social behaviors and, above all, they tend to be very tame, very amenable to handling, and as close to friendly as a lizard can get. With parental supervision and with parents assuming responsibility for their maintenance, subadult and adult bearded dragons make ideal children's pets, particularly the inland bearded dragon *(Pogona vitticeps)* and Lawson's dragon *(Pogona henrylawsoni)*.

All of the above qualities have contributed to bearded dragons becoming increasingly popular in the pet trade; many herpetoculturists are now working on large-scale propagation, as well as on establishing several morphs, particularly of the variable inland bearded dragon *(Pogona vitticeps)*.

The purpose of this book is to provide essential information to assure a high degree of success among the increasing number of dragon keepers in the United States and other parts of the world. Most of the information presented in this book is the result of the authors' ongoing work with these lizards since 1984.

HERPETOCULTURISTS & THE LAW

Many herpetoculturists (for good reasons) decry the restrictive, narrow-minded and short-sighted wildlife laws of Australia, that seriously limit the rights of Australian herpetologists and herpetoculturists. (Who would believe that the best breeders of Australian herpetofauna are German and U.S. herpetoculturists?) The fact is there are stringent international and national laws upholding these restrictions. Until they are changed (if ever), be aware that at the time of this writing it is illegal for a foreigner to collect and/or buy and remove from Australia any native wildlife. If you are an American citizen, being caught with illegal wildlife is a violation of Australian laws, of the Lacey Act and, depending on the species involved, possibly of CITES regulations, as well as the Endangered Species Act. This will assure you of a nightmare from which you may have difficultly recovering. There are really no good reasons for smuggling Australian reptiles. Many of the Australian species you may have dreamed of owning, including bearded dragons, are now bred in the U.S. on a commercial scale (from specimens initially exported from Europe). They can be purchased legally from breeders and pet dealers. The message here is, "Don't break the law. It isn't worth it, and it reflects poorly on all of us."

If you want to change existing wildlife and conservation laws (many of them are unsound and, in fact, may ultimately threaten the very survival of certain amphibian and reptile species), then do it legally by gathering information to substantiate your arguments, writing to your congresspersons, gathering signatures on petitions, campaigning, and exposing some of the flaws in existing wildlife laws, including those falling under CITES and the Endangered Species Act. In fact, some of the CITES regulations and their enforcement by various wildlife agencies, including U.S. Fish and Wildlife, are responsible for the deaths of thousands of amphibians and reptiles annually and may, indeed, endanger certain species rather than conserve them. With proper management, herpetoculture can become an important tool in conserving species, including many of the unusual localized forms of various amphibians and reptiles. In the case of many amphibians, including some Australian species, herpetoculture may in fact be the only hope for their survival into the next century.

GENERAL INFORMATION

WHAT'S IN A NAME?

Australians have given the popular name of dragon to the various members in the subfamily Agaminae of the large Old World family Chamaeleonidae that inhabit their country. (See Etheridge and Frost 1989 for the taxonomic system we are using; in most publications *Pogona* is a member of the Agamidae.) Of the approximately 50 or so agamine species in Australia, only certain members of the genus *Pogona* deserve the name "bearded dragon," because of their ability to extend the skin on the underside of the throat creating a beard-like display.

Until relatively recently, members of the genus *Pogona* were considered members of the genus *Amphibolurus.* One should also look under this genus when doing literature research.

AN OVERVIEW OF THE DRAGONS IN THE GENUS *Pogona*

The following species of *Pogona* are currently recognized:
Bearded dragon *(Pogona barbata)*
Lawson's or Rankin's dragon *(Pogona henrylawsoni)*
Pogona microlepidota
Western bearded dragon *(Pogona minima)*
Dwarf bearded dragon *(Pogona minor)*
North-west bearded dragon *(Pogona mitchelli)*
Nullarbor bearded dragon *(Pogona nullarbor)*
Inland or central bearded dragon *(Pogona vitticeps)*

THE BIG THREE

At the present time, only one species of bearded dragon *(Pogona vitticeps)* is firmly established in U.S. herpetoculture; two others, the bearded dragon *(Pogona barbata)* and Lawson's dragon *(Pogona henrylawsoni)* are bred in numbers too small to be able to determine whether the captive populations are increasing and self-sustaining. Nonetheless, these are the three species of bearded dragons currently kept and bred in the U.S. Although specimens of other species have been imported in the past, the small numbers imported, combined with their relatively smaller size (apparently not as appealing to hobbyists), have led to their not being established in U.S. herpetoculture.

which is only reliable with males. As mentioned above, because of the risk of injuring animals if performed by inexperienced individuals, we have chosen not to describe the procedure.

LONGEVITY

Based on our experience with bearded dragons, we estimate their longevity in captivity to be from four to ten years. We have had a male *P. vitticeps* specimen, obtained as an adult, for five years; we have had a female *P. vitticeps,* obtained as an adult (probably two years old), for seven years. We have had adult *P. barbata* pairs for more than five years. It seems reasonable to estimate that under good captive conditions the larger bearded dragons can probably regularly survive seven, possibly up to ten years in captivity. There is a longevity record of ten years and one month for an inland bearded dragon *(Pogona vitticeps)* and a record of nine years and eleven months for a male bearded dragon *(Pogona barbata)* acquired as an adult (Slavens 1992).

BEHAVIORS

Beard display: This defensive behavior is performed primarily by males and more readily during the breeding season, when the throat area darkens as a sex recognition and/or aggression display. It may vary from a slight extension of the "beard" to a full extension accompanied by an open display of the lining of the mouth, which will be a bright sulfur yellow in *Pogona barbata.* This species puts on the most impressive bearded display of all the dragons, followed by *Pogona vitticeps,* and possibly *Pogona nullarbor.* We have not noticed extension of a "beard" in *Pogona henrylawsoni.*

Arm waving: Juveniles of *P. barbata, P. henrylawson*i and *P. vitticeps* will perform an arm waving behavior, usually when basking, but also between periods of activity. During this behavior, the lizard stands on three limbs while one arm is waved at a relatively slow pace, making circles from back to front. In juveniles, this display appears to serve primarily for intraspecies recognition, but it may also function as an appeasement display towards larger specimens. As the animals grow older, this behavior usually disappears in males, but is retained by females, who use it as a form of appeasement behavior which is frequently performed during the breeding season (when males tend to be agressive), as well as during copulation.

Breeding behaviors: During breeding, the throats of males of *P. barbata* and *P. vitticeps* darken to nearly pitch black; this is a good indicator of sex. The throats of females in *P. barbata* and *P. vitticeps* also darken, but not to the same degree as males. Head bobbing, followed by copulatory attempts, will confirm the sex of male animals, as will occasional fights. As they fight, male

Female bearded dragon *(Pogona barbata)* **performing "arm-waving" behavior.**

Lawson's and inland bearded dragons resemble two small dinosaurs striking out, hissing with mouths open, bodies raised high above the ground and lashing out with their tails. Breeding behaviors in bearded dragons will prove to be reliable indicators of sex.

Basking behaviors: In *P. barbata* and *P. vitticeps,* it appears that dominant males will perch on the highest branches and basking areas of the enclosures. Though basking at high locations is often interpreted as a thermoregulatory behavior to increase body heat, in bearded dragons this may be a territorial behavior, as well as a means of avoiding the unusually high ground temperatures encountered in the wild. How this behavior relates to the reproductive success of males is worth investigating, including testing for the possible influence of temperature on fertility. When basking under a hot spotlight or in direct sunlight, bearded dragons may gape in order to cool down.

Digging under: We have noticed that bearded dragons will dig burrows and stay underground during the cool winter months and during periods of unusually hot weather.

SELECTION

At the time of writing, the only species of bearded dragon readily available in the trade is the inland bearded dragon *(Pogona vitticeps)*. The bearded dragon *(Pogona barbata)* and Lawson's dragon *(Pogona henrylawsoni)* are occasionally available in limited numbers.

Selection of potentially healthy animals will be critical to your success with these species. The following guidelines will help you select animals with a high probability of establishing in captivity.

SIZE SELECTION

Because most bearded dragons sold in the trade are captive-bred hatchlings or juveniles, one usually has little choice over size selection. As a general rule, juveniles at least two or three months old are a better choice for the beginning herpetoculturist. Some experience with proper supplementation of the diet of hatchling lizards is generally recommended if starting out with hatchling dragons. Without proper diet and vitamin/mineral supplementation, the risk of calcium deficiency in these lizards is quite high. Yearling animals, when available, are a very good choice and well worth the extra cost. If you are interested in breeding these lizards, our experience indicates that it is a very good idea to start with young animals. Larger, older females which may seem like a good deal (because they should be ready to breed right away) often are not. Female bearded dragons apparently have about three years of peak fertility, after which their breeding potential diminishes over subsequent years.

SEX SELECTION

If you are looking for one single pet, select a male bearded dragon. When in breeding condition, female bearded dragons may present a high risk of becoming eggbound if they are not bred. Furthermore, egg production exerts a toll on a female's energy reserves and health. Captive-raised single males probably have a better chance of living to a ripe old age than do single females.

NUMBER OF ANIMALS PER ENCLOSURE

There will probably be fewer problems if hatchlings and juvenile animals are raised singly. With proper vivarium design and meticulous attention to feeding schedules, young bearded dragons can be raised in groups, though they should eventually be segregated into smaller groups according to size.

In indoor vivaria, bearded dragons can be kept singly or in sexual pairs; also, in breeding groups consisting of one male and two or more females, depending upon enclosure size. In larger enclosures more than one male and several females can be kept together, though one should expect some fighting among males during the breeding season. We recommend indoor vivaria with a minimum floor space of 8 sq ft (2.44 sq m) for housing up to three large bearded dragons and at least an extra 4 sq ft (1.22 sq m) per each additional animal. See the **Breeding** section for information regarding problems likely to occur during the breeding season.

In outdoor vivaria, when maintaining bearded dragons in large groups, we recommend a minimum of 8 sq ft (2.44 sq m) of floor space per adult animal, preferably more.

SELECTION OF POTENTIALLY HEALTHY ANIMALS

1) Healthy bearded dragons are alert and active with clear, wide open eyes. Unless basking or sleeping, they will rest with the front part of the body raised above the ground between periods of activity. A bearded dragon which lies on the ground and does not demonstrate a wide-eyed state of alertness when picked up is probably not healthy. Check the animal for weight. The tail of a healthy animal will appear rounded; the outline of the hip bones will not be visible and the body will have a rounded appearance, without a lot of skin folds. A healthy bearded dragon gives the impression of vigor, good muscle tone and good weight when held in the hand.

2) Once you have picked out a potential purchase, ask that the animal be handed to you and examine it carefully. Make sure the tail is complete and all digits are present. If parts of digits and/or a section of tail are missing, realize that even though it may still be a healthy animal, this lizard will not regenerate these missing parts. Check the limbs. They should not demonstrate any unusual swelling(s). Examine the eyes to be sure they are clear and open wide. Check the edges of the mouth (particularly along the lower jaw) for any unusual swelling or crusting. Look at the underside of the lizard and inspect the area around the vent. Be sure there are no dried dark stains around the vent, indicative of diarrhea. Check for any unusual swelling in the area around the vent. Any lizard with runny, watery stools should be avoided.

3) After handling the lizard, check your hands for mites. If you find mites, the animal will have to be treated for them (if you are still planning to buy that particular lizard).

HOUSING & MAINTENANCE
OF BEARDED DRAGONS

ENCLOSURES

The authors are not proponents of "the-minimum-size-that-allows-for-survival" philosophy of reptile husbandry and vivarium design. Instead, we advocate a "minimum-requirements-that-allow-for-a-good-quality-of-life" philosophy, suggesting that a reptile have enough space for some exercise, some variation in landscape, and the opportunity to perform a variety of behaviors, including breeding.

INDOOR VIVARIA

Based upon the above standard, the authors consider the minimum size for keeping the larger bearded dragons to be a 72"Lx16"Wx17"H (182 cm x 41 cm x 43 cm) vivarium. The minimum size for keeping Lawson's dragons should be a 36"Lx16"Wx17"H (91 cm x 41 cm x 43 cm) vivarium, with a 48 in. (122 cm) long vivarium preferred.

There are currently several commercial all-glass vivaria with screen tops available in the general pet trade that are suitable for keeping bearded dragons.

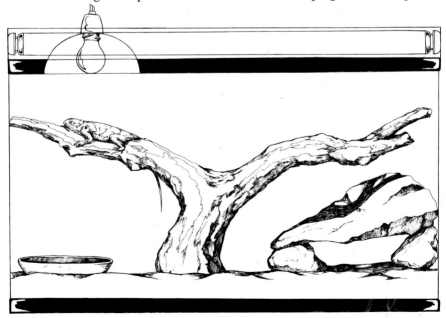

Basic indoor setup for a single bearded dragon. This should include sand as a substrate, an area for climbing, a shelter, a water dish, a spotlight for heat and full-spectrum fluorescent lighting. Drawing by Glenn Warren.

When available, aim for greater width in these vivaria. Some are now available with a 2 ft x 4 ft (61 cm x 122 cm) bottom surface. Because bearded dragons can be kept on a mostly dry substratum, other choices are available. One option is to build or have custom-built vivaria of wood or melamine with glass fronts. Some cabinet makers who specialize in designing reptile cages will build these to your specifications. Most have sliding glass fronts. Ventilation holes on the side or screened tops are highly recommended.

Another alternative is the open-top vivarium, which consists of a wood, melamine or fiberglass open box with an edge to prevent lizards from climbing out. The landscape is built up in the center. Lights are placed above the center part. If well designed, this type of vivarium can make a very attractive centerpiece in a room.

GREENHOUSES AND OUTDOOR VIVARIA
During the warm months of the year, many herpetoculturists keep their bearded dragons in outdoor vivaria with screen tops. This allows their animals exposure to direct sunlight and natural day length during the breeding season. Hatchlings and juveniles will also benefit considerably from the opportunity to bask in sunlight.

If several bearded dragons are kept together, an indoor setup large enough to allow for placement of an extra basking area is recommended.

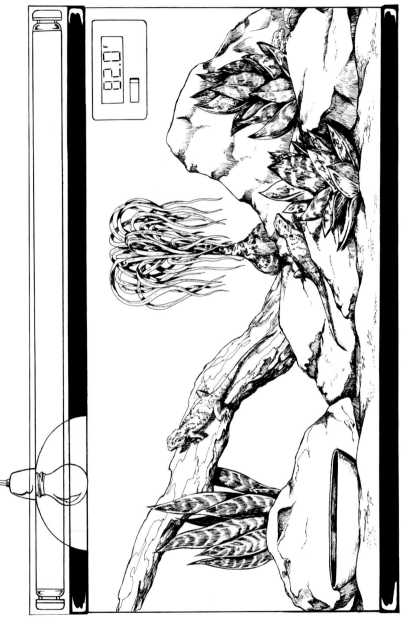

Naturalistic indoor vivarium for bearded dragons. Plants can be placed in pots concealed in the substrate or behind landscape structures. Ponytail palms, sansevierias, partridge aloes and small cycads can be used with these species. Fluorescent full-spectrum lighting running the length of the vivarium will be required in order for these plants to fare well. Drawing by Glenn Warren.

An indoor/outdoor vivarium made of melamine board with screen top. This vivarium can be wheeled indoors during inclement weather. It can also be taken outdoors to allow basking in direct sunlight. Photo by Pat Murphy.

Fiberglass-sided outdoor enclosures with screen tops. In areas with mild weather, such as southern California and south Florida, bearded dragons can be kept outdoors in this type of enclosure during most of the year.

Plastic tubs used for raising bearded dragon babies and fiberglass-walled enclosures for housing adults in a greenhouse with removable panels to allow exposure to direct sunlight.

Inside of one of the authors' multi-section greenhouse-type enclosures.

In warmer areas of the U.S., where there are no more than a few days of frost per year (such as southern California), bearded dragons can be kept in screenhouses or outdoor vivaria with screen covers during most of the year. During the winter they should be provided with supplemental heat and shelters, particularly if there are extended periods of cold, with daytime temperatures seldom climbing over 55°F (12.8°C). If the animals are to remain in these vivaria year round, the structures should be built so that the natural ground forms the bottom of the enclosures. The sides of the vivaria should extend one foot or more into the ground to prevent dragons from digging out. During winter and summer, the natural ground will allow the dragons to dig and hide in undergound shelters that will protect them from excessive heat and cold. Without the availability of a ground medium, dragons will not usually fare well outdoors on a year-round basis. Covering a section of outdoor vivaria with a 12-18 in. layer of loose alfalfa hay during the winter will provide bearded dragons with an insulated area for burrowing. In areas with winter rains, outdoor vivaria should be covered to afford the animals protection.

In outdoor vivaria, the substrate will need to be cleaned and changed on a regular basis <u>and</u> as needed. If the ground forms the substrate, it will have to be raked every few weeks to remove dried fecal matter. It is a good idea to

A small, easily moved, screen-sided enclosure used by the authors for raising baby bearded dragons. This type of enclosure allows for daily exposure to sunlight.

replace a 2-3 in. (51-76 mm) layer of the ground in outdoor vivaria once a year. An alternative is to turn over the top 10 in. (25.4 cm) of soil. As with indoor vivaria, landscape structures should be washed (using at least a high-pressure hose), water containers should be cleaned and plants watered as needed. Temperature and heating systems should be monitored daily.

Note: Outdoor vivaria are not recommended for bearded dragons in areas of considerable rainfall unless they are set up inside covered and well-ventilated greenhouses. Bearded dragons inhabit relatively dry, often semi-arid areas, with primarily seasonal summer rains and will not fare well in damp environments. *Pogona barbata* is the species most adaptable to environments with high relative humidity.

Gas heater used by the authors to heat one of their greenhouses.

Basic design for a bearded dragon greenhouse. The sides are hardware cloth or aluminum screening. The bottom is framed by redwood board which extends 1 ft (30.5 cm) into the ground and 1 ft (30.5 cm) above the ground. The purpose of the above-ground board is to discourage dragons from climbing up the screen and to prevent them from escaping when the door is opened. The below-ground board is to prevent dragons from digging out. As an alternative, hardware cloth or fiberglass sheeting can be extended from the bottom frame 1 ft (30.5 cm) into the ground. The door should be set above the redwood board. The roof should be a greenhouse-type, corrugated semi-translucent fiberglass roofing. During the winter, the screen sides can be covered with clear plastic sheeting and a heating system installed to provide supplemental warmth. Greenhouse/screenhouse-type setups work best in areas of milder climate. Drawing by Glenn Warren.

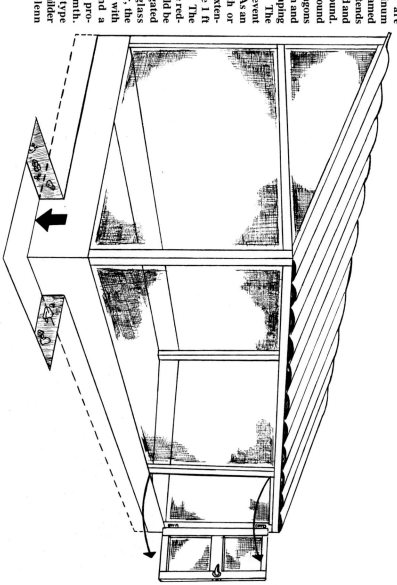

- 19 -

SUBSTRATES

In a basic vivarium setup without live plants, a fine silica sand (no finer than #30) can be used as a substrate, or you can obtain sand made up of fine decomposed granite. Fine aquarium gravel or pebbles can also be used. If you wish to use live plants with bearded dragons, it is a good idea to simply bury live plants in pots in the substratum and conceal the pots with rocks or wood. An alternative, which will work only in large setups, is as follows: On the bottom, place a 1.5-2 in. layer of pea gravel or small pebbles for drainage. Then add a 2-3 in. layer of a barely moist mixture consisting of 50% good quality potting soil mix without perlite and 50% coarse sand. Above this mixture, place a 1 in. layer of silica sand or a fine grade smooth gravel. In this type of setup, plants can be removed from their pots and placed directly in the sandy soil substratum. To minimize excessive digging of the upper layers, some rocks and/or sections of driftwood or cholla skeleton should be used in the landscaping. The plants should be carefully watered at their base using either a pump-type sprayer or a baster. Naturalistic vivarium designs work best with large setups, at least 48 in. (122 cm) long for *P. henrylawsoni* and at least 72 in. (183 cm) long for *P. barbata* or *P. vitticeps.*

LANDSCAPING

All bearded dragons climb. Bearded dragon are semi-arboreal and commonly bask or lie on branches; in Australia, they commonly bask on fence posts. In vivaria, basking and resting areas should be created which consist of large rocks and some diagonally-placed sections of cork bark (sold as cork rounds) or wood sections. In addition, shelters should be made available, placed out of range of the intense heat of basking lights. Formed concrete shelters are now commercially available, as well as clay shelters, plastic shelters, and sections of cork bark.

Live plants in pots can also be used. Recommended plants are: Snake plants *(Sansevieria*; many species and varieties are available), ponytail palms *(Beaucarnea recurvata),* small palms and dracaenas. Outdoors in greenhouses, the authors have had success with elephant bush *(Portulacaria afra)* and jade plant *(Crassula argentea),* as well as acacia trees grown with their trunks slanted, all planted directly in the ground.

COVER

A screen cover is recommended for keeping these species, though they will not readily climb out of tall vivaria with smooth sides. Screen covers will keep out children and pets, allow for the placement of lights, and prevent the escape of both dragons and food insects. All outdoor vivaria should <u>always</u> be enclosed and include a screen top. Cats, raccoons, opossums, skunks and birds of prey will find bearded dragons tasty treats.

LIGHTING

All bearded dragons kept indoors will require at least one spotlight over each basking area. See **Heating** section below. In addition, full-spectrum lighting (such as Spectra Lite® or Vita-Lite®) is highly recommended. These bulbs produce some UVA but insignificant amounts of UVB, the ultraviolet radiation believed to allow many lizards to synthesize vitamin D3 required for the absorption of calcium. Many herpetoculturists also recommend having a single BL (not BLB) type blacklight turned on for a few hours each day. This type of bulb generates high levels of UVA (a lower frequency of ultraviolet radiation than UVB), which may be beneficial to some lizards and may positively affect reproductive success in some species. A protective shield should be used with BL type lights to reduce UVA exposure to human observers. Currently, full-spectrum bulbs generating a higher level of UVB are reportedly being developed specifically for use with reptiles, to enable them to synthesize their own vitamin D3. These should prove extremely beneficial for bearded dragons.

In spite of the above recommendations, bearded dragons can be raised under only incandescent light, if careful attention is paid to other husbandry factors, particularly quality of diet, including vitamin/mineral supplementation. Nonetheless, whenever possible, exposing bearded dragons to direct sunlight for at least 30 minutes three times a week is highly recommended, particularly when rearing hatchlings and juvenile animals. Sunlight will contribute significantly to the prevention of calcium deficiency. Indeed, regular exposure to sunlight is often the only cure for the shakes and tremors (symptoms of calcium and vitamin D3 deficiency) often reported in hatchlings and juveniles. Exposure to sunlight should be to direct sunlight, not sunlight shining through glass, which filters out UVB and can raise the temperature inside a vivarium enough to kill animals. A shaded area and shelter should <u>always</u> be made available when exposing animals to direct sunlight. We recommend placing small dragons in cages constructed of wood with shade cloth sides or in plastic tubs with a shade cloth cover.

HEATING

Temperature: In a vivarium, the daytime temperature should be 80-85°F (26.7-29.4°C), with one or more basking areas where the temperature reaches 88-95°F (31.1-36.7°C). At night the temperature can safely drop to 70°F (21.1°C). See the section on **Breeding** for winter pre-breeding conditioning temperatures.

PRIMARY HEATING

When these lizards are kept in indoor vivaria, the primary heat source should be an incandescent bulb or spotlight, in a reflector-type fixture, placed above a basking area (usually located toward one end of a vivarium) to allow for creating a temperature gradient within the enclosure. In larger vivaria, a basking area can be designed in the center or two different basking areas can be set up. Generally, this type of lighting will create a heat gradient whereby the closer a lizards gets to the light source, the warmer it will be. The wattage of the bulb should be selected to create a temperature of 88-95°F (31.1-35°C) (check with a thermometer) in the section of the basking area closest to the light. The light and fixture should be placed above the screen cover or at a height well out of reach of the lizards, to prevent the possibility of thermal burns. Care must be given to placement of the light, so that no flammable portion of the vivarium or the surrounding area is exposed to direct (or near) contact with the bulb. Also, the fixture should be secure enough to prevent the light unit from falling or moving from its position. Think fire prevention.

A recently available alternate heat source is a ceramic infrared-element bulb by Pearlco®, which produces heat without light. These bulbs have a high heat output; a 60 watt infrared bulb will produce adequate warmth for most bearded dragon vivaria. They should be used in conjunction with fluorescent full-spectrum bulbs.

SECONDARY HEATING

In cold areas, supplemental heat can be supplied at night with an infrared-element bulb, subtank heating pads or low wattage red incandescent bulbs. These should be on timers set to come on at night. A thermostat is preferred to a timer (in the case of certain subtank heaters); a rheostat may be a better choice. With outdoor vivaria, pig blankets (large fiberglass enclosed heaters) or infrared-element bulbs can be placed inside insulated shelters for heating on cold nights and during winter. They should be placed on thermostats to prevent the possibility of overheating. Always follow manufacturers' instructions with any heating system or thermostat to prevent the risk of fire. In areas where daytime temperatures during the winter seldom rise above 40°F (4.4°C) and nighttime temperatures are seldom above freezing, keeping bearded dragons in outdoor vivaria is definitely not recommended, even with appropriate heating systems. If the heat fails, you risk losing your animals. The only type of outdoor systems that can be recommended under such conditions are greenhouses heated with gas heaters or other greenhouse heating systems. These should be wired to an alarm system to warn the owner in case of heater failure so that an alternate emergency heating system can be used.

Heating outdoor vivaria

In outdoor vivaria, heat is normally provided by the sun, either directly or as a result of a greenhouse effect from sunlight passing through glass or fiberglass. In greenhouse-type setups, ventilation and movable panels are necessary in order to prevent overheating during the summer. In warm areas screenhouses are recommended over greenhouses because they minimize the risk of overheating and allow direct exposure to sunlight. During the winter, gas heaters, spotlights, infrared-element bulbs and/or pig blankets (fiberglass enclosed heating elements) can be used as sources of supplemental heat (see Secondary heating above).

Thermometers

A thermometer should always be used to accurately monitor temperatures in vivaria, primarily to prevent the "cooked reptile syndrome." ("How could I have known that a 100 watt bulb over a ten gallon vivarium would be too hot for my baby dragons? See, they look like little mummies!") Human estimates of vivarium temperatures are often way off (sometimes dangerously so). There are now several kinds of inexpensive thermometers sold in the pet trade; there is no good excuse for not owning one.

For serious herpetoculturists, the authors recommend the use of continuous reading, electronic digital thermometers with an external probe to monitor the temperatures in vivaria and in incubators. These can be purchased at electronic supply stores (e.g., Radio Shack) or ordered from mail order scientific supply companies (e.g., Edmund Scientific). For greenhouses and outdoor vivaria, there are several large dial-type minimum/maximum thermometers that also work well.

Smoke alarm
Note: A room containing vivaria should be installed with a smoke alarm.

Ventilation
Vivaria for bearded dragons should have good air flow. Indoor vivaria should have screen covers or screen sides.

Maintenance
The enclosures of bearded dragons should be maintained on a regular basis. For indoor vivaria, feces should be scooped out once each week. The substrate should be replaced when it becomes too soiled. Landscape features should be removed, washed and disinfected when soiled, at least every one to two months, more frequently if many animals are kept together. The glass of the

vivarium should be cleaned every one to two weeks. Water should be changed and/or provided regularly. The water containers should be disinfected when fouled. Plants will need to be watered on a regular basis. On occasion they will need to be replaced. Temperature and heating systems should be monitored on at least a daily basis.

For outdoor vivaria, the substrate will need to be regularly cleaned and changed as needed. If the ground forms the substrate, it will have to be raked every few weeks to remove dried fecal matter. It is a good idea to replace a 2-3 in. layer of the ground of outdoor vivaria once a year. As with indoor vivaria, landscape structures should be washed using at least a high-pressure hose. Water containers should be cleaned and plants watered as needed. Temperatures and heating systems should be monitored daily.

An outdoor fiberglass-walled enclosure. One side of the roof consists of translucent corrugated panels. The other side is screened. The bales of hay are used as resting areas in the summer. In the winter hay is spread out, serving as insulation.

FEEDING BEARDED DRAGONS

The majority of dragons sold in the pet trade are captive-bred juveniles and immature animals. Most owners are unwilling to part with their adult bearded dragons. The following feeding regimens and schedules will result in rapid growth and a high survival rate of captive-bred juveniles.

FOOD SOURCES

Bearded dragons can be raised and maintained on commercially-bred house crickets *(Acheta domestica)*, mealworms *(Tenebrio molitor)*, king mealworms *(Zophobas morio)*, and mice. These food animals can all be readily obtained from stores specializing in reptiles or mail order suppliers advertising in herpetocultural publications. All plant foods can be obtained from your local market.

THE IMPORTANCE OF FEEDING PREY ANIMALS A HIGH QUALITY DIET

This point cannot be over-emphasized: Any food animals offered to bearded dragons need to be fed a high quality diet. A standard procedure is to maintain crickets and/or mealworms on a high quality diet of pulverized rodent chow, high quality flaked baby cereal or (better yet) the high calcium/vitamin D3 cricket diet manufactured by Ziegler Brothers. Sliced oranges should be provided to crickets as a source of water; similarly, for mealworms carrots should be offered. Once they are removed from their enclosures, insects should be offered to the bearded dragons as soon as possible. In this way, the insects should still be "gut-loaded" (herpetocultural term) at the time of feeding, meaning they will still be full of the high quality diet, including vitamins and minerals, they have recently been fed. For the same reasons, unweaned mice (pinkies or fuzzies) should be offered soon after removal from their mothers.

FEEDING REGIMENS

HATCHLINGS UP TO TWO MONTHS

Two- to three-week old crickets (up to 3/8 in. (9.5 mm)) should be offered two to three times a day, offering only what the animals can eat at one feeding. Young lizards can become stressed by excess crickets climbing on them. In addition, any supplementation on the excess crickets will usually be gone by the time a well fed lizard decides to feed again.

For the first feeding of each day, the crickets should be vitamin/mineral supplemented. Every other day offer a small amount of very finely chopped kale and frozen chopped mixed vegetables (corn, carrots, green beans and peas, thawed). Note: Do not feed larger insects to small dragons (see Partial paralysis associated with hind leg extension under **Diseases & Disorders**).

TWO MONTHS TO FOUR MONTHS

Three- to four-week old crickets (1/2 in. (12.6 mm) or less) should be offered twice a day (no more than they will eat at one feeding) and just molted mealworms (only 1-2 per animal) once a day. Insects should be vitamin/mineral supplemented one feeding every other day. Offer a dish of finely chopped greens (kale, mustard greens, collards) and finely chopped mixed vegetables every other day.

FOUR MONTHS OLD TO SEXUAL MATURITY

Offer once to twice daily, four- to five-week old crickets; also, mealworms, king mealworms and (optional, every one to two weeks) newborn to five-day-old mice, depending on the size of the dragon. Insects should be vitamin/mineral supplemented every other day. Offer chopped greens and chopped thawed mixed vegetables every other feeding.

ADULTS

Adults should be offered four- to six-week old crickets and/or king meal-worms *(Zophobas morio)* every one to two days. King mealworms can constitute one third to one half of the diet of adult *P. barbata* and *P. vitticeps*. In areas which have not been sprayed with pesticides or other agricultural chemicals, field-collected grasshoppers and locusts (when available) will be relished by bearded dragons. Pink and/or fuzzy mice or just weaned mice can be offered once a week. Insects should be vitamin/mineral supplemented two feedings a week. Offer chopped greens (kale, mustard greens, collards) and thawed mixed vegetables every other feeding.

During the breeding season females should be offered a high quality diet rich in calcium and vitamin D3. Live just-weaned mice offered to adult females two to three times a week will assist females in getting back into condition quickly following egg-laying.

Note: Some herpetoculturists feed mice to adult dragons as a primary diet, but the long term health effects of this type of diet have yet to be determined. The authors suspect a risk of bearded dragons becoming obese on a diet with a high percentage of pink and fuzzy mice, and recommend just weaned hoppers (which have a lower fat content) instead. Until further research is done, the authors recommend that a varied diet be offered to bearded dragons.

VITAMIN/MINERAL SUPPLEMENTATION
This is of critical importance when raising bearded dragons. Inadequate supplementation, together with inadequate diet, are considered by many to be primary causes of rearing problems and mortality among juvenile bearded dragons. Although there is ongoing research in this critical area, the best courses of action remain unknown. The following are methods that have worked for the authors.
1) Feed all food insects a quality diet.
2) Provide vitamin/mineral supplements.

SUPPLEMENTATION SCHEDULES
Supplement insects one feeding per day for juveniles up to two months and one feeding every three days for adults and subadults with the following powdered mix: one part reptile or bird multivitamin/mineral supplement to two parts vitamin D3/calcium supplement (with no vitamin A), such as RepCal® or Nekton MSA®. To dust the insects, place the mix in a jar, introduce the insects and gently swirl so that they become coated. One of the goals of this mix is to cut down on the high levels of vitamin A found in many commercial vitamin/mineral supplements, which may be toxic and detrimental to the successful rearing of juveniles. We have also had good results with a mix of 50% Osteoforme® and 50% powdered calcium carbonate.

SUMMARY OF SUPPLEMENTATION SCHEDULES
Juveniles up to two months: Supplement insects one feeding per day.
Subadults and adults: Supplement insects one feeding every three days.

ADDITIONAL CONSIDERATIONS
NOTE ON FEEDING AND SIZE OF FOOD ITEMS
As a general rule, offering hatchlings and juveniles a number of small food items several times a day, rather than a few larger ones less often, results in faster growth. Because of their greater relative surface area, smaller food items tend to be digested faster. During the course of a day, a lizard can eat small food items a number of times. However, if a large prey item has been eaten, the animal's gut may be filled with a slowly digesting meal, leaving it less likely to go after another large food item. Smaller food items will move through the digestive tract at a faster rate, leaving room for more to be consumed. Large prey items also increase the risk of a fatal condition associated with spastic extension of hind legs (see **Diseases and Disorders**).

MUTILATION PREVENTION: THE IMPORTANCE OF REGULAR FEEDING WHEN KEEPING JUVENILES IN GROUPS
Many a dragon keeper maintaining hatchlings and juveniles in groups has

been horrified when confronted with a cage of mutilated juveniles, an event which may happen literally overnight. Sometimes the mutilation phenomenon just creeps up on someone. "Oh, a lizard lost the tip of its tail. Oh, well, no big deal. Oops, another lizard lost the tip of its tail. I wonder what's going on. And there a lizard has lost some toes and part of its tail, and here's another one...and another one." The fact is that juvenile bearded dragons, if overcrowded and underfed (particularly *P. henrylasonii*, but also *P. vitticeps*), will nip off parts of tails and even toes of enclosure mates. Bearded dragons grow fast and require a lot of food initially. They are also competitive; larger specimens may intimidate smaller ones and, if food is lacking, may consider a nip here and there. This tendency usually disappears by four months; we have not noticed it in larger animals. The lesson here is: Keep those baby dragons well fed.

THE NEED TO SEGREGATE BY SIZE WHEN REARING LARGE NUMBERS OF BEARDED DRAGONS

During at least the first four months, *Pogona* juveniles should be segregated by size. Larger specimens will compete more effectively for food and thus will grow considerably faster than smaller specimens. As the size discrepancy increases, smaller dragons will become more intimidated and feed relatively less than larger ones, resulting in even greater size discrepancies. Small

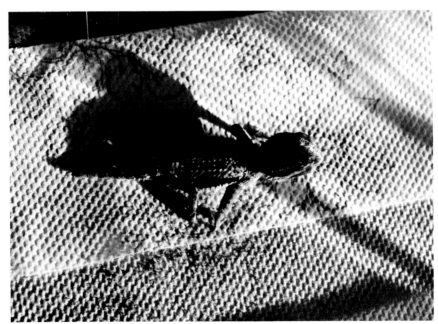

A juvenile Lawson's dragon which has been mutilated by conspecifics. Note the missing hand, foot and section of tail. Baby bearded dragons need to be fed several times a day to prevent the occurence of these mutilation incidents. Specimens should also be segregated by size.

specimens are also more likely to become subject to the tail and toe mutilations mentioned previously.

LEG TWITCHING, SHAKES, PARTIAL PARALYSIS

These symptoms are commonly reported in juvenile bearded dragons and are indicative of calcium deficiency; lack of vitamin D3 and calcium, as well as inadequate calcium-to-phosphorus ratios must be considered as possible causes of these symptoms. However, even herpetoculturists who are very meticulous with their lizards have seen these symptoms in juveniles of all *Pogona* species. One possible cause, which has been proposed by Dr. Larry Talent of the University of Oklahoma, may be excessive vitamin A supplementation. Preliminary research suggests that too much vitamin A may be toxic and may impair calcium metabolism in some lizard species. With vitamin/mineral supplements that contain too much vitamin A, increasing the dosage in an attempt to correct a calcium deficiency may result in increased symptoms. If these symptoms appear, use <u>only</u> calcium/vitamin D3 supplements with <u>no</u> vitamin A, such as Reptical® or Nekton MSA® or whatever new brand may appear on the market. In addition, allow daily exposure to at least 30 minutes of sunlight. In most cases, hatchlings or juveniles with these symptoms will recover after a few days of exposure to sunlight.

The propensity of baby bearded dragons to develop these symptoms seems to vary among clutches, several breeders reporting these symptoms to be more common in first clutch offspring and last clutch offspring in a given breeding season. Several dragon breeders, including the authors, suspect that the propensity for developing these symptoms may be linked to the diet and health of the mother, suggesting that a deficiency in the female may lead to a greater likelihood of deficiency in its offspring. The dietary regimen before and/or after hibernation, plus how soon a female breeds following removal from hibernation (brumation) may be important factors in the frequency of these symptoms in the offspring from a particular clutch. By the same token, a female laying its fourth, or in some cases fifth clutch of the season may be stressed because of the nutritional demands of such a high reproductive rate. This is an area warranting further investigation.

MORTALITY RATES

Bearded dragons have a significant mortality rate during the first four months of life, with the highest mortality occurring during the first two months following hatching. In our experience, *Pogona barbata* is more difficult to raise than *P. henrylawsoni* and *P. vitticeps*. Mortality rates prior to sexual maturity have varied between 28% and 45% in various clutch groups that we have kept back for breeding. *Pogona henrylawsoni* and *Pogona vitticeps* have proven generally hardier, with mortality rates prior to sexual maturity of between 9% and 24% in various clutch groups.

WATER

Clean water should be offered three times a week in a shallow water dish or pan. Plastic jar lids or deli container lids will work well with hatchlings. Small plant saucers (used under pots) will work well with adults. The water container should be shallow enough for animals to bend their heads down into the container from a normal stance. In most areas, tap water will be adequate for dragons, but use bottled drinking water if the quality of your water is doubtful. Do not use distilled or purified water, as a small amount of dissolved minerals may be beneficial. It is very important that the water be clean. Whenever the water is fouled, the container should be disinfected with a solution of 5% household bleach in water, thoroughly rinsed and refilled. Like many other lizard species, dragons will often defecate in their water containers. For this reason it is recommended that water be made available for only a few hours at a time, preferably in containers small enough to discourage this behavior. Water fouled by the feces of sick animals can be a primary vector for the spread of gastroenteric disease. It is a good idea to regularly disinfect water containers.

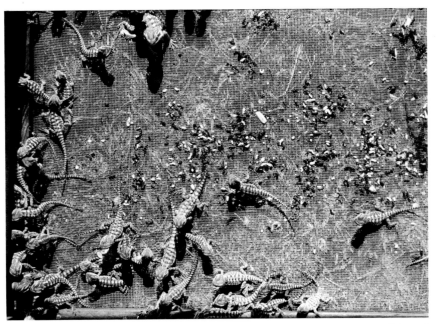

A group of Lawson's dragons kept in a screen-sided enclosure. Daily exposure to sunlight and frequent feedings are required to raise baby dragons successfully.

HANDLING

Regular handling for short periods and interaction with your animals (e.g., hand feeding) can lead to a more rewarding relationship with them. Many herpetoculturists will carry their dragons on their shoulders or arms. Do <u>not</u> do this outdoors unless you are in an area surrounded by a solid wood fence or other solid barrier. Bearded dragons can suddenly dash off your body; if this happens in the street you are facing a possibile dragon roadkill. It is recommended that you <u>not</u> take your dragons out in public, other than at a proper forum for such displays, such as a herpetological show. Many people are afraid of reptiles and may become quite frightened if they happen upon an animal in the open, even if it is on someone's shoulder. <u>Use good judgment</u>.

Bearded dragons are among the best of lizard pets. Unlike most lizards, they readily tolerate brief periods of handling and are not skittish. They are generally calm and seem to behave in an almost friendly manner.

BREEDING

We have successfully bred members of the genus *Pogona* both indoors, in all-glass vivaria, as well as in custom-built greenhouses, heated by gas heaters. At the onset of our breeding project, we speculated that it would be necessary to expose the animals to a reduced-temperature range, and a reduced photoperiod, as preconditioning for breeding. This approach turned out to be quite successful and we feel it is critical to the long term, sustained breeding of these lizards. We have also kept specimens outdoors, in southern California, in pens, without supplemental heating.

CONSIDERATIONS BEFORE ATTEMPTING TO BREED BEARDED DRAGONS

If one is interested in breeding bearded dargons (they often will breed whether you are interested or not), the following should be considered:

1) The animals you are attempting to breed must be healthy. This means they should have good weight and demonstrate no symptoms of disease.

2) You must have at least one adult sexual pair.

3) It is very important that you maintain breeding dragons (particularly females) on a high quality diet. There is research currently in progress which suggests that the diet of female lizards can have a significant effect on their offspring and possibly on subsequent generations. Herpetoculturists are currently concerned with the effects of excess vitamin A and insufficient vitamin D3 on offspring and lack of calcium in the diet of females. Although optimal breeding fitness in female lizards has not yet been determined, some factors would seem to be large size and good weight (not obesity), combined with good muscle tone. Age also seems to be significant; our experience suggests that female bearded dragons of the three species we have focused on will breed best (optimal egg production) during their second, third and fourth years and breed less efficiently thereafter.

SEX RATIOS

The authors keep groups consisting of several males and several females in large enclosures. In indoor vivaria, a single male can be kept with several females and breed successfully. It is a good idea to have an extra male and switch males in order to assure high fertility. If the vivarium is large, two or more males can be kept with several females, but one can expect quite a bit of fighting during the breeding season. Crowded conditions may be detrimental to successful breeding. An enclosure should allow for dispersal of subdominant males with enough space for a male to breed undisturbed. On the other hand, the presence of more than one male in a vivarium may stimulate a male to breed more. An alternative is to set groups of one male and several females in several vivaria in such a manner that each male will be within the others' field of vision. They will bob at each other and attempt to attack each other through the glass (getting all fired up) all the while maintaining a safe distance.

With the inland bearded dragon *(Pogona vitticeps)* in particular, there are cases where males kept with females in relatively small enclosures will constantly attempt to copulate with females to the point that the back of the neck area of females becomes seriously damaged and the females become quite stressed. When this occurs, the animals may have to be separated. Use your judgment.

PREBREEDING CONDITIONING

Our standard procedure for indoor prebreeding conditioning is to set all lights on timers and reduce the daily photoperiod to 10 hours of daylight and 14 hours of darkness. The heat light wattage is reduced so that the temperature of basking areas closest to the lights is 75-80°F (23.9-26.7°C), while the

A gravid female Lawson's dragon. Successful breeding of this species appears to be diminishing. This suggests either inbreeding depression or long-term effects of inadequate diets.

vivarium temperature away from the lights is significantly cooler. Other secondary heat sources are set on timers so as to turn off at night. We allow the night temperatures to drop down to 60° ± 4°F (15.6 ± 2.2°C) but bearded dragons will safely tolerate temperatures in the low 50's°F (10-12°C). Depending on the conditions, feeding by dragons will be significantly reduced or absent during the cooling period.

The reduced heat and photoperiod schedule is initiated during the first two weeks of December and runs through February 15, at which time both heating and lighting schedules are returned to normal, with a lighting schedule of 14 hours of daylight and 10 hours of darkness. Some herpetoculturists initiate the cooling and reduced photoperiod schedule as early as mid-October, returning to a normal schedule by January 15. For animals kept in greenhouses in southern California, we set the heaters to go on at 60°F (15.6°C) and the animals are simply exposed to the natural photoperiod of the locale.

Note: Herpetoculturists living in the southern hemisphere should adjust the authors' recommended breeding schedules accordingly.

BREEDING
Within three to four weeks of return to normal conditions, behaviors relating to breeding will be evident, including aggressive displays and fighting between males, submissive displays of females and copulation. Bearded dragons are offered food daily during the period between return to normal conditions and the onset of breeding behaviors. This allows animals that are thin following hibernation to gain weight prior to actual breeding. Females should be maintained on an optimal feeding schedule throughout the breeding season which can extend until the end of summer.

EGG-LAYING
Gravid females will appear and feel significantly more plump by the time they are ready to lay their eggs. The bearded dragons in our setups will often dig several burrows before they consider one suitable for egg-laying. Under indoor conditions, we recommend that females be transferred to enclosures with a sandy garden soil. Pure sand, because it will not readily bind together, will make the digging of a burrow difficult; it is important to provide an alternative substrate with moderate cohesiveness. Some herpetoculturists simply moisten the sand at one end of the vivarium, but in our experience most females offered this type of environment will fail to create what they consider a suitable burrow and will not readily lay eggs. We have found the following method works well: when a gravid female dragon is noticed digging around, we dump a couple of buckets of freshly dug garden soil into the vivarium. We

A gravid inland bearded dragon digs an egg-laying burrow while a male looks on.

Female inland bearded dragon next to egg clutch (excavated by the authors).

then pat it down so that it binds together and by hand begin to dig out an opening (or two) to simulate the entrance of a burrow. Often a gravid female will use that opening, complete a burrow and subsequently lay her eggs. We feel that failure to provide a suitable substrate for egg-laying can result in a female being reluctant to lay eggs, which increases the risk of egg-binding.

Our records indicate that actual egg-laying with most specimens occurs between 1 pm and 6 pm. When egg-laying occurs, a female will be almost completely concealed within the burrow, with only the tip of her head visible at the entrance. Because we keep most of our animals in greenhouse setups, we mark the general area so that we can locate the eggs once the female has finished laying.

EGG INCUBATION
After the female has completed laying, the eggs are carefully dug up and removed from the egg-laying site and transferred to incubators. Before introducing the eggs, we place a layer of moistened vermiculite (about 5 parts coarse vermiculite to 4 parts water by weight) on the bottom of the incubator. We use styrofoam poultry incubators, such as the Hovabator®. The incubator is calibrated for 84°F (28.9°C) by adjusting the wafer-type thermostat.

The process of properly adjusting incubator temperature requires at least six hours. We recommend that the incubator be properly calibrated at least 12 hours before the eggs are introduced in order to make sure the incubator maintains the proper temperature. This procedure is done with the use of an electronic digital thermometer with a probe (available at Radio Shack and through Edmund Scientific, as well as other electronic supply companies). The probe is set inside the incubator; the switch is set to outside reading (through probe). This will give a continuous readout of the inside incubator temperature which makes it invaluable for herpetoculturists. With this type of thermometer, the temperature of a unit such as the Hovabator® can be controlled without opening the incubator, simply with a slight turn of the thermostat adjustment.

Note: It is important that the incubator be kept in a room cooler than the desired incubating temperature, particularly during summer heat waves. Remember that commercial incubators heat but do not cool, so they cannot drop the incubator temperature below the ambient air temperature. Also, exposure to high temperatures (above 90°F (32.2°C)) is more likely to kill the developing embryos than brief exposures to cooler temperatures.

Incubation cabinet set up by the authors. The unit is heated by four 75 watt bulbs, controlled by a thermostat.

Large numbers of hatchling bearded dragons can easily be maintained in plastic tubs, heated by individual spotlights.

After the incubator has been properly calibrated, the eggs are introduced singly on their side, burying about two thirds of the egg, with about one third of the egg surface showing above the vermiculite. The eggs should not be moved or turned once in place. During incubation, the eggs and the vermiculite should be inspected daily. Adding a small container of water inside the incubator can be helpful in maintaining high relative humidity. Depending upon the moisture level of the vermiculite, the eggs and the medium will need to be misted lightly about once a week. Under the above conditions, the eggs of *Pogona barbata* will hatch in 69-79 days, the eggs of *Pogona henrylawsoni* will hatch in 45-54 days, and the eggs of *Pogona vitticeps* will hatch in 55-75 days. In most clutches, eggs will hatch within 24 hours of the first hatching, but in others hatching may extend over as long as six days.

Although we have not kept careful records on failed hatchings, we estimate that between 15 and 25% of eggs failed to hatch. Upon opening, some of these eggs proved to be infertile, while others died at various stages of embryonic development.

Within the twenty-four hours prior to hatching, an egg will show a slight but noticeable loss of turgidity and collapse of the shell due to reduced internal pressure. Healthy, vigorous animals will usually slit the egg (with an egg tooth located at the tip of the snout) within a few hours following this initial collapse. Some will take longer, while others (presumed to be weak) will fail to slit the egg shell. As a rule, we incise any collapsed eggs (see below) of a given clutch that are not slit within twenty-four hours of our noticing the initial collapse. If eggs that have been collapsed for about twenty-four hours are incised, a small percentage of juvenile lizards that emerge may survive. To incise an egg, fine scissors (such as cuticle or embroidery scissors) are used to very carefully cut a small slit (1/4 - 1/3 in. (6.4-8.5 mm)) through the center, running lengthwise along the upper surface of the egg. The slit should run the center third of the length of the egg. Note: Allowing the scissor point to penetrate significantly beyond the shell layer can injure or kill small lizards, so extreme care is required for this process. Once the egg is slit, leave it alone. In time, a lizard may emerge on its own. Never manually pull a lizard from its egg following incision of the shell. For several reasons, including failure to allow time for complete absorption of the yolk and difficulties in adjusting to breathing outside air, manually removing an unhatched lizard usually results in its death. In our experience the survival rate of lizards which fail to slit the egg shell on their own yet do emerge following incision is low.

Once the hatchling lizards have completely emerged and are active within the incubator, they can be removed and transferred to a small rearing container, such as a standard twenty gallon vivarium, and raised according to the instructions provided in this book.

LONG-TERM BREEDING

Large-scale breeders should keep careful records of the egg production by respective females. Our records indicate that female bearded dragons have about three years of peak breeding, after which egg production significantly diminishes. Captive-bred animals should be kept back and raised up every two to three years to replace aging animals.

HATCHLING WEIGHT & SIZE COMPARISON			
Species	Weight	Snout/Vent Length	Total Length
P. barbatus	.08 oz (2.21 gm)	1.6 in (40 mm)	3.76 in (94 mm)
P. henrylawsoni	.06 oz (1.75 gm)	1.4 in (35 mm)	2.2 in (55 mm)
P. vitticeps	.13 oz (3.6 gm)	1.7 in (43 mm)	4.4 in (110 mm)

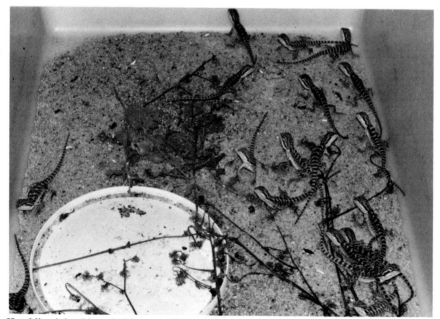

Hatchling inland bearded dragons (*Pogona vitticeps*).

Inland bearded dragon female with hatchling, pictured to show size relationship. Photo by Pat Murphy.

Lawson's dragon mother with offspring. Photo by Pat Murphy.

DISEASES AND DISORDERS

Captive-bred bearded dragons raised in isolation from other lizard species tend to be very hardy and not very susceptible to disease.

BEFORE TAKING AN ANIMAL TO A VETERINARIAN

In our experience, careful consideration is suggested before taking a lizard to a veterinarian. We highly recommend that you investigate whether a veterinarian is experienced with lizards before you make an appointment for a sick dragon. A veterinarian lacking experience with reptiles can cost you lots of money and can kill your animal.

A good general rule is not to wait until your animal appears really sick to take it to a veterinarian. The best time to take it is when it appears a little off, but still has a significant amount of vigor. Sick and weak lizards, particularly smaller animals, usually do not survive. An example of when to take a bearded dragon to a veterinarian is when the animal appears healthy and eats, but does not gain weight and has runny stools. In these cases, fecal exams often reveal a gastroenteric infection or parasite problem that can be readily treated.

Another good rule when taking a reptile to a veterinarian is to set a limit on what you want to spend. We recommend that you state that limit (at the beginning of treatment) to the veterinarian, who should then be able to advise you accordingly. Tests and treatments can often amount to many times the original cost of an animal. Sometimes a tentative treatment, without the high cost of certain tests, may be a sound course. At times a veterinarian may recommend treatment which might be unreasonable. We have been told of one case involving suggested treatment of a respiratory infection using aminoglycoside antibiotics. To assure proper hydration, the veterinarian wanted to keep the animal in the clinic. Total costs for treatment would have been several hundred dollars. The individual decided to increase enclosure temperature as treatment instead and the animal's respiratory infection cleared up. A rule which we abide by is that if a dragon is too weak to move and open its eyes, we euthanize it or allow it to die on its own. Ultimately, any decision on these matters concerning your animal is up to you.

LOSS OF TAIL AND/OR DIGITS

Parts of tails or digits of juvenile bearded dragons are sometimes nipped off by conspecifics. Unlike many other lizard species, caudal autotomy or dropping of part of the tail is not part of the defensive repertoire of these species. Once lost, neither tail nor digits will grow back. Fortunately, infections seldom develop following these cannibalistic snacks.

MITES

While most bearded dragons sold in the pet trade will initially be mite free, they may contract mites from other species when kept in mixed collections. In the long run, mites can increase to the point of deleteriously affecting the health of these lizards. When present, mites will usually be noticed as tiny bead-like creatures crawling about the lizards, often in the neck area. The most effective treatment consists of removing infected lizards from their enclosures and treating them in separate enclosures with No-Pest® strips or other insect-killing strips impregnated with 2.2 dichlorovinyl dimethyl diphosphate. In small enclosures of 20-55 gallons, we use a 1/2 in. x 2 in. (1.27 cm x 5.1 cm) section for twelve hours, partially covering any open screened areas to reduce air flow. If mites are still present, we allow the strip to remain another twelve hours. The treatment is repeated after 9 days. The original enclosures are emptied and thoroughly cleaned with a 5% bleach solution. All basking areas, shelters, dried woods, etc., are replaced or soaked in a 5% solution of bleach in water for at least 30 minutes and then rinsed thoroughly before being returned to the enclosure.

With hatchlings and up to half-grown animals, we avoid using pest strips, but instead rinse the animals daily under water, keeping them in simple bare enclosures that also can be washed out daily. After two weeks of methodical washing, the mites are usually gone.

When treating dragons kept in outdoor enclosures, the enclosures from which they are removed for treatment are also treated with one or more pest strips for at least three days. The treatment is repeated in 9 days after having once again removed all animals. Basking areas, shelters, etc., are treated as noted above.

Fortunately, the great majority of dragon owners will not usually have to contend with mites.

INTERNAL PARASITES
Weight loss, worms in the stools, runny stools, listlessness and gaping are all possible symptoms of internal parasites. Have a stool sample examined by a veterinarian and follow the recommended treatment if any of these symptoms are present.

PREVENTION OF CALCIUM DEFICIENCY
Juvenile bearded dragons grow at a remarkable rate and consequently require large amounts of usable calcium in their diets in order to build their fast growing skeletal systems. Under most captive conditions, the following factors are required in order for calcium to be absorbed into the blood stream:

1) Calcium should be present in the diet, preferably in the form of calcium carbonate or calcium gluconate.

2) The ratio of calcium to phosphorus should be at least one part calcium to one part phosphorus; preferably two parts calcium to one part phosphorus.

3) Vitamin D3, either synthesized by the animal as a result of exposure to sunlight or administered as a dietary supplement, is required in order for calcium to be absorbed.

By following the instructions on maintenance and feeding in this book, you should not have problems with calcium deficiency.

SYMPTOMS OF CALCIUM/VITAMIN D3 DEFICIENCY

One of the initial symptoms of calcium/vitamin D3 deficiency in juvenile bearded dragons usually is tetanic twitching or the "shakes." Other symptoms may include neurological problems and soft jawbones. Treatment consists of supplementing the diet with a calcium/vitamin D3 supplement (not a general vitamin/mineral supplement) and exposing the animal to sunlight for at least 30 minutes daily. Exposure to sunlight is considered by many to be the most effective way of dealing with these symptoms, which suggests that a vitamin D3 deficiency may be the primary cause, since herpetoculturists typically provide enough dietary calcium.

RESPIRATORY INFECTIONS

Compared to most lizards, members of the genus *Pogona* tend to be rather resistant to respiratory infections. Nonetheless, prolonged exposure to temperatures that are marginally cool, but not quite cold enough to induce brumation, can result in respiratory infections. When present, the most obvious symptoms are gaping, forced exhalation of air, puffing of the throat and a puffed up appearance of the body. In severe cases, mucus will accumulate in the mouth and may emerge from the nostrils. Usually, keeping the animals at higher temperatures, with daytime highs in the upper 80's to low 90's °F (30.5-33.8°C), will allow bearded dragons to fight off these infections. If the symptoms persist, the animals should be taken to a veterinarian and treated with injectable antibiotics. In our experience, exposure to higher temperatures is often effective. Note: Large numbers of nematode parasites may also cause gaping in bearded dragons. Also, do not interpret the normal gaping behavior of bearded dragons when they are overheated as a sign of respiratory infection.

GASTROENTERIC INFECTIONS

If your dragons are showing loss of appetite, weight loss and listless behavior, accompanied by loose, discolored and/or smelly stools, then you should have a fecal exam performed by a veterinarian as soon as possible. The cause will very likely be some type of gastroenteric infection. Once diagnosed, many types of gastroenteritis are easily and successfully treated, as long as you do not procrastinate in seeking veterinary help.

PSEUDOMONAS

Life threatening *Pseudomonas* infections occasionally turn up in breeder's collections. If your animals are showing signs of weight loss, loss of appetite, and runny stools, have a stool exam performed by a qualified veterinarian. He or she will then be able to recommend an appropriate treatment.

COCCIDIA

These protozoa will turn up in breeders' dragon colonies, particularly if their animals are kept with other species of lizards or if new animals are introduced. The only way to determine the presence of coccidia is to take a stool sample to a veterinarian. As a rule, if lizards are showing signs of losing weight and have consistently loose, runny and smelly stools, they should have their stools examined by a qualified veterinarian.

EGG-BINDING

Several factors can lead to egg-binding in captive bearded dragons, including weakness associated with illness, dietary factors (such as calcium deficiency), low weight or obesity, and inability to find a suitable egg-laying site. The first step is to establish the probable cause and attempt to rectify the condition(s). If the animal appears ill or thin, then it should be taken to a qualified veterinarian who may diagnose the cause. A veterinarian can also administer vasotocin, which may induce egg-laying. In some cases, surgery may be required to save the animal. If you suspect that the animal may be reluctant to lay eggs because of the lack of a suitable egg-laying site, then follow the fresh-garden-soil method mentioned under **Egg-laying**.

PARTIAL PARALYSIS ASSOCIATED WITH HIND LEG EXTENSION

Spastic hind leg extension has long been considered a symptom of calcium deficiency. However, on numerous occasions we have noticed this occuring the day after feeding large prey (crickets or king mealworms) to small dragons. Animals that appeared healthy one day demonstrated hind leg extension the next day and in most cases eventually died. Large bulky prey affects the nervous system (spinal nerves) of bearded dragons in some way. We do not know the actual cause of death. Warning: Do NOT feed large prey items to juvenile dragons.

NOTES ON SPECIES

BEARDED DRAGON *(Pogona barbata)*

This is the classic bearded dragon of herpetological literature. Small numbers have been exported from Australia, and there are relatively few in U.S. collections. The authors first obtained this species as German-bred juveniles in 1984. Difficulties in rearing hatchlings, a somewhat slower growth rate than *P. vitticeps,* and difficulties in consistent long-term breeding have prevented this species from being firmly established in U.S. herpetoculture. Despite what some may believe, this is not *P. vitticeps* in different clothing. It is a much more shy species, readily adopting cryptic behaviors, such as lying along the length of a branch, limbs close to the body, head stretched along the branch, and not moving. The coloration of this species is also duller and more cryptic than *P. vitticeps.*

As a pet, although *Pogona barbata* will be tame, they do not usually demonstrate the outgoing fearless personality of *P. vitticeps* and *P. henrylawsoni.* However, this species does put on the most striking "bearded" display of any lizard, showing off the sulfur yellow of its open mouth in the process. In the authors' experience, this is also the most cold-hardy of the three species of *Pogona* that are bred in the U.S. The authors have kept them in outdoor pens in southern California without supplemental heat. Night temperatures during the winter often dipped into the 40's°F (4.5-9.4°C) and very occasionally into the upper 20's°F (-1.7 to -3.3°C). The animals spent a good deal of the winter underground, in burrows, emerging in March (remember this is the San Diego area of southern California that we refer to). Generally, the authors would recommend this species for more experienced keepers <u>only</u>. *Pogona barbata* seems to be more tolerant of high relative humidity than *P. vitticeps* and thus may be a better choice in locales where humidity levels could pose a problem.

Distribution: This large bearded dragon occurs in eastern and southeastern Australia, excluding the Cape York Peninsula and Tasmania (Cogger 1992). It is a semi-arboreal lizard which can be found in a wide range of habitats from coastal wet sclerophyll forests to inland arid scrubs.

Variation: Although this widely distributed species is said to be quite variable in Australia, specimens in the U.S show little variation.

Size: Total length, up to nearly two feet. The following chart indicates the lengths of adults in our breeding colony.

Age to sexual maturity: Under optimal conditions, this species will be sexually mature by 10-18 months of age. Captive-raised species will breed at one to two years from hatching, depending upon rearing conditions.

ADULT SNOUT-VENT & TOTAL LENGTH COMPARISON			
P. barbata	All Adults	Males	Females
Snout Vent Length	6.4-8.6 in (159-216 mm)	6.6-8.6 in (165-216 mm)	6.4-8.1 in (159-203 mm)
Total Length	14.7-19.3 in (368-482 mm)	15.2-19.3 in (381-482 mm)	14.7-17.3 in (368-432 mm)

Secondary sexual characteristics: It is almost impossible to reliably sex juvenile animals of this species. All adult males have significantly larger and wider heads when compared with females. Males are also slightly larger, though less heavy-bodied, than females. The throat area of males darkens when mature, becoming darker during breeding season. Females' throats also darken, yet not to the same degree. Males' tails appear somewhat wider at the base and taper more gradually than do those of females. Males have significantly larger preanal and femoral pores. Attempts at sexing juveniles are usually based on assessing slight differences in the degree of tail taper.

Maintenance: Bearded dragons can be maintained like other *Pogona*. They should have large branches placed diagonally as climbing and resting sites. A minimum-size vivarium for one pair should have a 48 in. x 24 in. (182.9 cm x 40.6 cm) floor area, preferably larger.

Breeding: See chapter on **Breeding**. The following charts indicate the authors' breeding results for 1985 and 1986.

CLUTCH SIZES & LAYING DATES -- P. BARBATA -- 1985			
	Clutch #1 Date / Eggs	Clutch #2 Date / Eggs	Total Eggs
Female #1	Apr 26 / 21	Jun 6 / 18	39
Female #2	May 24 / 19	Jun 17 / 21	40
		Total	79

CLUTCH SIZES & LAYING DATES -- P. BARBATA -- 1986				
	Clutch #1 Date / Eggs	Clutch #2 Date / Eggs	Clutch #3 Date / Eggs	Total Eggs
Female #1	Mar 4 / 30	Mar 30 / 35	Apr 27 / 25	80
Female #2	Feb 27 / 17	Mar 1 / 23		40
Female #3	Apr 1 / 24			24
Female #4	Apr 8 / 12			12
			Total	156

Note: Females 3 and 4 were subadults when purchased. 1986 was their first breeding.

LAWSON'S DRAGON OR BLACK-SOIL BEARDED DRAGON
(Pogona henrylawsoni)

Formerly known in herpetoculture as Rankin's dragon, this species has an interesting history. It first became available out of Germany in 1984. The first specimens sold in the United States were offered by Ron Tremper, under the name Rankin's dragon, as a new soon-to-be-named species, probably *Amphibolurus rankini*. Ron was correct that it was a new species, but he was wrong on the eventual name. It would be years before the Rankin's dragon of herpetoculture would be acknowledged by herpetologists. Indeed, when the 1986 edition of Harold Cogger's *Reptiles and Amphibians of Australia* was published, many herpetoculturists expected to find the infamous Rankin's dragon, but such was not the case. At that time, impatient herpetoculturists, instead of calling this species *Amphibolurus sp.*, decided they would stay with *Amphibolurus rankini*. Later, when lizards of the *Amphibolurus* complex were broken up, *Amphibolurus rankini* was included with members of the genus *Pogona* and became *Pogona rankini* of herpetoculture. Unbeknownst to many, Rankin's dragon had, in fact, been described in 1985 (Wells). It is now officially *Pogona henrylawsoni*..

Lawson's dragon, unlike some of the other members of the genus *Pogona* doesn't really qualify as a bearded dragon, because this species does not display a "beard." It does have the same docile, almost friendly personality of *Pogona vitticeps*. One advantage of this species is that it does not get nearly as large as the bearded dragons and will fare well in smaller enclosures.

Size: The following chart represents the size range of adults in the authors' breeding colony.

ADULT SNOUT-VENT & TOTAL LENGTH COMPARISON			
P. henrylawsoni	All Adults	Males	Females
Snout Vent Length	5-6.1 in (124-152 mm)	5-5.8 in (124-146 mm)	5.1-6.1 in (127-152 mm)
Total Length	9.2-12.2 in (230-305 mm)	10.2-12.2 in (254-305 mm)	9.2-11.4 in (230-286 mm)

Age to sexual maturity: *Pogona henrylawsoni* will be sexually mature by one year of age under optimal rearing conditions.

Sexing: It is almost impossible to reliably sex immature animals of this species. Adult males have slight jowls, and they are proportionately less heavy-bodied than females. During the breeding season, the sexes can usually be identified by their respective sexual behaviors. Males will perform aggressive displays and behaviors towards each other and will attempt to court and mate with females. During the breeding season, the heavy-bodied gravid females will be easily recognized.

Distribution: Black-soil plains of central Queensland, Australia.

Variation: This species displays relatively little variation in color, though some may be more maroon instead of a dull brown. There is little genetic diversity in United States captive populations, and it is possible these populations will experience problems, including decreasing reproductive success. This situation is not likely to change unless Australia reconsiders its wildlife laws and allows export of new stock.

Maintenance: Essentially the same requirements as other *Pogona*.

Breeding: See chapter on **Breeding**.

The following charts show breeding results by the authors during 1985 - 1986.

CLUTCH SIZES & LAYING DATES -- P. HENRYLAWSONI -- 1985

	Clutch #1 Date / Eggs	Clutch #2 Date / Eggs	Total Eggs
Female #1	May 21 / 21	Jun 18 / 22	43
Female #2	Jun 7 / 18		18
Female #3	Jun 17 / 21	Jul 15 / 18	39
Female #4	Jul 3 / 20		20
		Total	156

CLUTCH SIZES & LAYING DATES -- P. HENRYLAWSONI -- 1986

	Clutch #1 Date / Eggs	Clutch #2 Date / Eggs	Clutch #3 Date / Eggs	Clutch #4 Date / Eggs	Total Eggs
Female #1	Mar 23 / 21	Apr 18 / 19	May 11 / 17	Jun 17 / 21	78
Female #2	Mar 15 / 25	Apr 13 / 20	Jun 1 / 18		63
Female #3	Mar 26 / 19	Apr 26 / 12	May 28 / 23		54
Female #4	Mar 20 / 17	May 31 / 18			35
Female #5	Mar 25 / 14	Apr 19 / 15	May 15 / 18	Jun 12 / 19	66
Female #6	Apr 3 / 20	Apr 24 / 22			42
Female #7	Apr 16 / 20				20
Female #8	Apr 25 / 19				19
Female #9	Sep 28 / 16				16
Female #10	Died gravid				0
				Total	393

Variations in numbers of clutches and clutch size in P. henrylawsoni can be partially attributed to age. Females 7 and 8 were obtained in 1985 as subadults. Females 9 and 10 were born in late August, 1985, and thus were gravid at 1 year of age.

A group of inland bearded dragons in one of the authors' outdoor screenhouses. A gravid female in front is performing "arm waving," an appeasement behavior, in response to the black-throated male to her right.

This example of an open-top indoor vivarium is kept in a science department lab at White Mountain Junior High School in Rock Springs, Wyoming. Photo by Kaye McCarron.

Gold head/light iris morph of *P. vitticeps*. Photo by Corey Blanc.

Red head morph hatchling inland bearded dragon and hatchling red morph (red head and body).

A group of inland bearded dragons during the breeding season. Note the tails curled up in a manner similar to curly-tailed lizards *(Leiocephalus)*. This behavior appears to be associated with a certain state of "alertness" or "arousal." Photo by David Travis.

Egg-laying: a female Lawson's dragon finds a suitable spot.

Egg-laying: the female begins to excavate a burrow.

Egg-laying: she lays her eggs. Only the top of the snout can be seen at the entrance to the burrow.

Egg-laying: she exits the burrow, covers the eggs and fills the burrow. Eventually any signs of egg-laying will be invisible, so it is important to mark the site when egg-laying behavior is noticed.

The eggs are carefully excavated.

A clutch of 20 Lawson's dragon eggs.

Bearded dragons hatching in one of the authors' incubators. A Hovabator®, calibrated to maintain a temperature of 84°F (28.9°C) was used. Note collapsing of eggs prior to hatching.

Juvenile red phase inland bearded dragon. The reddish coloration becomes noticeable by two months of age.

OTHER ANIMALS

Very large enclosures (preferably room-size) will be required to keep other animals with bearded dragons. We have had good success keeping the following species with bearded dragons in our greenhouse-type enclosures.

Amphibians: White's tree frogs *(Litoria caerulea)*

Reptiles: Frilled lizards *(Chlamydosaurus kingii)*, blue-tongue skinks *(Tiliqua scincoides)*, ridge-tailed monitors *(Varanus acanthurus)*, Baja blue rock lizards *(Petrosaurus thalassinus)*, veiled chameleons *(Chamaeleo calyptratus)*, and Morrocan uromastyx *(Uromastyx acanthinurus)*.

Note : Not all of the species mentioned above were kept with bearded dragons at the same time.

One key to the successful keeping of other species with bearded dragons is an enclosure with plenty of space, so that the animals do not trample each other. The White's tree frogs in our greenhouse, for example, would spend most of the day on jade plants. The frilled lizards would spend most of their time in trees. The uromastyx had a set area with burrows. Indoors, only large custom-made enclosures would allow you to combine several species.

Inside greenhouse-type enclosures containing bearded dragons, veiled chameleons *(Chamaeleo calyptratus)* can be kept on small trees.

White's tree frogs (*Litoria caerulea*) resting on jade plant in the authors' screenhouse which also houses bearded dragons. Large planted enclosures with a sizable water container are required in order to combine species in this manner.

Moroccan uromastyx (*Uromastyx acanthinurus*) and young bearded dragons. The authors have successfully bred this species under these conditions. Note the "pig blanket"-type heater (red) on the right.

Ridge-tailed monitor *(Varanus acanthurus)* with bearded dragon. This small monitor is bred in small numbers by European hobbyists and is occasionally available through specialist reptile dealers.

One of the authors' frilled lizards *(Chlamydosaurus kingi)* which lives primarily on tree branches in a screenhouse that contains a breeding group of bearded dragons *(Pogona barbata)*.

REFERENCES

Badham, J.A. 1976. The *Amphibolurus barbatus* species group (Lacertlia: Agamidae). Aust. L. Zool 24: 423-443.

Greer, A. 1989. The Biology and Evolution of Australian Lizards. Surret Beaty and Sons Pty Limited. 264pp.

Cogger, H. 1992. Reptiles and Amphibians of Australia. Comstock/Cornell 775pp.

De Vosjoli, P. 1991. The right way to feed insect eating lizards. Advanced Vivarium Systems. 32 pp.

De Vosjoli, P. and R. Mailloux. 1987. The Art of Dragon Keeping: Husbandry and Propagation of *Amphibolurus barbatus* and *Amphibolurus rankini* in Proc. of the N. Cal, Herp. Soc. 1987 Conference On Captive Propagation and Husbandry of Reptiles and Amphibians, pp. 57-66.

Hoser, R. 1993. Smuggled. Apollo Books, Sydney, Australia.

Slavens, F.L. and K. Slavens. 1992. Reptiles and Amphibians in Captivity: Breeding - Longevity and Inventory. Woodland Park Zool. Gardens. Seattle WA. 497 pp.

Wells, R.W. and C.R. Wellington. 1985. A Classification of the Amphibia and Reptilia of Australia. Aust. J. Herp. Suppl. Ser. No. 1:1-61.

SOURCES

Cricket diet: Ziegler Bros., Inc.
        P.O. Box 95
        Gardners, PA 17324